Please return/renew this item by the last date shown on this label, or on your self-service receipt.

To renew this item, visit **www.librarieswest.org.uk** or contact your library

Your borrower number and PIN are required.

Libraries**West**

First published in 2018 in Great Britain by
Barrington Stoke Ltd
18 Walker Street, Edinburgh, EH3 7LP

www.barringtonstoke.co.uk

This story was first published in a different form as
Design a Pram (Egmont Books Ltd, 1991)

Text © 1991 & 2018 Anne Fine
Illustrations © 2018 Vicki Gausden

A CIP catalogue record for this book is available
from the British Library upon request

ISBN: 978-1-78112-736-0

Printed in China by Leo

This book is in a super readable format for young readers
beginning their independent reading journey.

PramBusters!

Anne Fine

With illustrations by
Vicki Gausden

Barrington Stoke

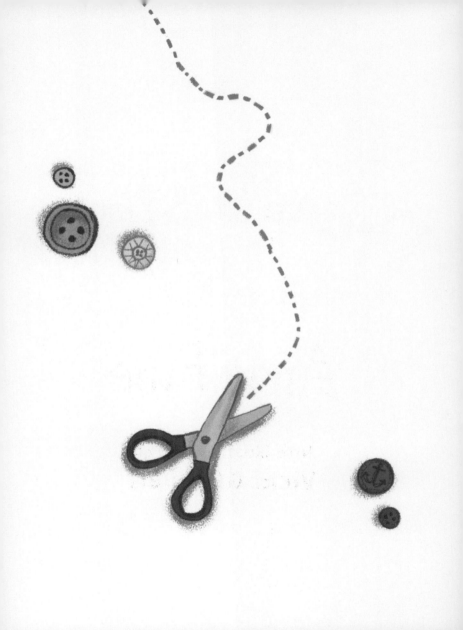

Contents

Chapter 1

The Box of Surprises

My name is Malik. In the summer I go to a holiday day camp. It's out of town, on a farm. A minibus comes to pick us all up each morning. Except for Hetty. Hetty lives on the farm next door to the camp, so each day she comes on her pony, Peppo.

Hetty ties Peppo to a fence. He's in the shade and has a bucket of water. We all get off the minibus and go over to pat his nose. We pull fresh grass out from under the hedge to feed him.

Peppo watches us. He flicks his tail at the flies that bother him. Sometimes he makes a funny whickering noise.

"He's bored," Hetty tells us. "But if he were at home, he would be even more bored, standing in the field."

We're never bored at summer camp. We play ball games and run races. We learn how to do outdoor things like make a camp fire, and tie strong knots. We sing songs we know, and learn some new ones. We play tag.

After snack-time, Mrs Hope and Mr Oakway take turns to sit in the big wooden chair that looks like a throne, and read us stories and poems. (Mrs Hope is going to have a baby soon, so she has more turns sitting in the throne chair.)

Sometimes we make things out of the bits and pieces in the Box of Surprises. Mrs Hope and Mr Oakway collect things all year to put in the box. All sorts of empty rolls and boxes. Tissue paper. Odd bits of ribbon. Buttons. Shiny bright paper. Little bags of confetti. Pots of glitter. Anything and everything!

Some people might call it 'playing with junk', but we call it 'junk modelling' and we all love it.

We all sit down outside, in a big circle.

"Here are the paper clips and glue sticks and rubber bands," Mrs Hope says. "Over there are the felt-tip pens and scissors. Choose a few bits that you like out of the Box of Surprises and make something interesting."

No one is ever quite sure how to start. But then one of us gets up and digs in the Box of Surprises. Maybe we pick out a strange shiny coin and an empty plant pot with tiny holes in the bottom. And a handful of bright pink straws and a lonely green shoe lace.

After you've looked at the things in your pile for a while, you get the start of an idea.

Perhaps the straws will fit in the holes in the bottom of the plant pot. Then the plant pot might look a bit like an alien from a faraway planet. The lonely green shoe lace could be the alien's best scarf. And if you glue the coin onto his front, as if he had one big round shiny eye, then ...

Off we go!

We make a bit of a mess, but it's easy to clear up outside. One day, when the wind was blowing hard, we asked Mrs Hope if we could move the Box of Surprises into the barn and make our junk models there.

"I'm sorry," Mrs Hope said. "But the farm animals use the barn in winter. If we leave some of our bits and pieces stuck in the straw by mistake the cows might eat them."

So when it rains and we have to move inside the barn, we only ever get to use the pencils and felt-tip pens. And even then Mrs Hope and Mr Oakway check to make sure we put all the pen tops back on, and haven't left any lying around on the barn floor.

Chapter 2

Rain, Rain, Nothing but Rain

One day it rained. It was already
raining when we piled into the minibus.
It was still raining when we reached day
camp. It was so wet that Hetty even left
Peppo at home in his warm dry stable
and walked over the field with her mum
and a big umbrella.

Rain, rain. Nothing but rain.

It rained so hard that Mrs Hope and Mr Oakway told everyone, "Quick! Run to the barn."

Once we were all inside, we sang a
few songs and we took turns to show
off our cartwheels and somersaults and
handstands. (The barn's not big enough
for proper races.) Then Mrs Hope
handed out sheets of white paper and
felt-tip pens in all different colours.

That's when the grumbling began.

"We've nothing flat to rest our paper
on."

"Just all these lumpy bales of straw."

"The tip of my felt pen is making holes in my paper."

"The ground's so bumpy, I can't colour in."

Mr Oakway sighed. He looked around the barn. In one corner lay two smooth flat bits of wood. (The farmer had just

put in a new kitchen, and this wood had been left over.)

"We'll borrow these," said Mr Oakway.

He laid the bits of wood flat on the straw bales. They made a very big table.

We gathered round and then the grumbling got worse.

"Your elbow's in my face."

"You're crumpling the edge of my paper."

"Watch out! You let your pen roll over my picture."

Mrs Hope said, "This won't do! Everyone is getting in everyone else's way."

"I know," Mr Oakway said. "I'll tape the sheets of paper together. Then you can choose something to draw, and do it as a group."

We started to argue about what to choose. Sarina said, "I think we should draw animals."

Robbie said, "No. Cars and vans and lorries."

Harneesh said, "I only like to draw patterns."

Miriam said, "I'm good at houses and trees."

I had a brilliant idea. "I know! Let's split up into two teams. We can move the tables apart and have two really big bits of paper, not just one. Mrs Hope can choose what we draw. Both teams will draw what she picks and the best drawing at the end will be the winner."

"Yeah!" Oscar said. "A real competition!"

"But who will choose the winner?" asked Tyler.

"I will," said Mr Oakway.

We didn't dare start grumbling again, but we weren't pleased. Mr Oakway is hopeless at choosing. Just hopeless. He's too nice. In fact, he's such a softy he always ends up saying something like, "But they're so good that they'll all have to win."

That's no use, is it? Not in a
competition. No, it's not.

Chapter 3

Picking the Teams

That day, there were twelve of us at the camp all together, not counting Mrs Hope and Mr Oakway.

"That will be perfect," said Mr Oakway. "It makes exactly six of you at each table."

Sarina asked, "But how will we pick the teams?"

"I know," Bartosz said. "Let's do what we used to do back in my old school in Poland. We chose someone to pick, and the rest of us sat on the floor in a circle. The person we chose had to shut their eyes and walk round the circle three times."

Sarina asked, "Why?"

"So they forgot where their friends were sitting."

I asked him, "What happened after that?"

"That was the good bit," Bartosz said. "The person walked round the circle again, still with their eyes shut. But this time they had to pat a few people on the head. And those people made up the first team."

"I get it," Sarina said. "And everyone who was left was on the other team."

"That's right," Bartosz said. "It's a good way to pick teams."

"I think whoever picks today should wear a blindfold," Hetty said firmly. "Or they might peep."

"Or trip, and open their eyes by accident," said Mr Oakway. (I told you he was a softy.)

So Mrs Hope found a strip of flowery tea towel in the Box of Surprises and made a blindfold. And we tossed dice to see who would get to wear it and pick the teams.

I got three fives and a four, so I did pretty well. Nineteen! But Nancy got three sixes and a four. Twenty-two! So Nancy was the person who had to choose the teams.

We sat in a circle and kept very quiet. Mrs Hope put the blindfold on Nancy, and she walked round the circle three times. Then she walked round again and began to pat heads.

She patted Tyler's and Oscar's heads.
Then she patted Bartosz's.

"Are you sure you're not looking?"
said Tyler. "So far, you've only picked
boys."

"Sssh!" we all hissed.

Nancy ignored him. She had two more to pick, and she picked Kristy and Layla. Then she pulled off the blindfold.

"Who's in my team?" she asked.

They all stood up – Kristy and Layla and Tyler and Oscar and Bartosz.

So all the rest of us knew that we were in the other team. But Mr Oakway called our names out anyway. It was me (Malik) and Miriam and Harneesh and Sarina and Robbie and Hetty.

Nobody grumbled. We all thought that seemed fair enough.

Chapter 4

Draw Me a Pram

Mr Oakway made one massive sheet of paper for each team. We shared out the felt-tip pens and asked Mrs Hope, "So what shall we draw?"

She said, "I know! Draw me a pram."

"She thought of that idea because she's going to have a baby soon," Hetty whispered.

But Mrs Hope heard. "That's right," she said to Hetty. "I reckon I'm about to pop."

We all laughed. "What sort of pram shall we draw?" I asked Mrs Hope.

"Any sort, Malik," Mrs Hope said, with a smile. "Just draw the sort of pram you would have loved back when you were a baby."

We all looked at one another. I can't remember back when I couldn't walk or talk. I certainly can't remember back to when I sat in a pram!

"We'll just have to guess," I told everyone.

"Right," Mr Oakway said. "Two teams, on different sides of the barn. The team that draws the pram a baby would like best will be the winners."

We smiled and nodded. But we all know Mr Oakway is such a softy that he can never choose a real winner. We knew he'd end up saying something like, "But they're so good that they'll both have to win."

He always does.

Chapter 5

PramBusters!

"Right," Hetty said. "We'll talk in whispers. If we talk loudly, the other team will hear, and pinch our bright ideas."

"What bright ideas?" Harneesh asked.

Hetty gave him a beady look. "The ideas we're going to have. We're going to draw a pram that any baby would be proud to sit in. It will be comfy and interesting and educational. It will be the best pram in the world and the baby won't ever want to get out of it."

"Then it should have furry sides and a waterbed mattress," Robbie said. "My aunty has a waterbed and she says it's so soft it's like lolling about on a cloud."

"Brilliant," we all agreed. "A waterbed mattress."

"The pram should have a mobile," Robbie added. "I had a mobile over my cot when I was a baby. It had tiny golden whales and silver dolphins that swirled round above my head. My dad says that I loved it."

"OK," we all agreed. "A mobile with golden whales and silver dolphins."

"Music!" Harneesh said. "Babies love music. So when the wheels on the pram go round, they could wind up a musical box that plays gentle songs."

"Good idea!" we all told him.

"And the pram should smell nice," Sarina said. "We could have something that clips on the side. Then the baby can squeeze it to puff out the smell of warm milk and cookies." She clapped her hands together. "Oh, I know we're going to win. This is exactly the sort of pram that any baby would love."

"Yes!" said Harneesh. "We're really good at this!"

Sarina smiled. "PramBusters!"

"Yes," we all agreed. "We are the
PramBusters!"

I had an idea. "How about a display
of swirly stars for the baby to look at
when it's being pushed home on a dark
night?"

"Yes," Miriam said. "And we will
need sharp knives sticking out of all four
wheels to keep away fierce dogs."

We turned to stare at Miriam.

Miriam stared back.

Chapter 6

Miriam Storms Off

I was the first to speak. What I said was, "Miriam, did we hear right? Did you just say our pram should have knives sticking out of all four wheels?"

"That is disgusting!" Harneesh said.

"And dangerous," Sarina agreed. "Our pram could cut a fluffy little puppy to ribbons by mistake."

"No, it couldn't," said Harneesh. "Because we are NOT using Miriam's idea."

"Sssh!" Robbie warned. "The other team will hear us, and steal our ideas."

"They're welcome to steal that one," I said. "Because we definitely don't want it! Harneesh is right. It's disgusting!"

Now Miriam was in a huff. "If my very first idea is so disgusting, maybe I shouldn't be in this team at all! Maybe I should be on the other team."

I didn't care. "Maybe you should!" I snapped.

"All right, then," Miriam said. "If that's how you feel, I'm going!"

Before anyone could stop her, Miriam got up and marched across the barn to ask Mrs Hope and Mr Oakway if she could please leave us, and swap with someone in the other team.

Chapter 7

The Other Team's Pram

The other team were busy with an argument of their own. And none of them were whispering, so I heard all of it.

"What we want," Oscar was saying, "is a really good computer back in the baby's house. Then the parents can sit at home and press the arrow keys on the keyboard to drive the pram."

"Or use a joystick," Kristy said. "Like pilots in planes."

"Yes," Oscar said. "Whichever works best to make the pram go forwards and backwards, and to the left and right."

Nancy said, "The pram will need to go around corners too. And it will need a webcam on the front, so the parents can check where it's going."

"And rockets at the back," said Layla. "So it can go at high speeds."

"With retro brakes," Kristy added, "so it can stop in no time.'

Oscar said, "That means our pram will have to be very thin and pointy, like a jet plane."

"But what about the baby?" Tyler complained. "If the pram's thin and pointy, like a jet, the baby will be squashed in at the sides."

"It won't mind," said Oscar. "A pram that goes as fast as a jet plane is the sort of pram that any baby would love."

"And we could give it something to play with," Kristy suggested. "How about a gamma ray gun? Then it could shoot anyone who was sneaking up on it."

"Or a button it can press that puffs out poisonous smoke."

That's when Tyler lost his temper.

"Stop calling this baby 'it'," he shouted. "Babies aren't 'it'! They're 'he' or 'she'. Little boys or little girls. And they're far too young to be out on their own in a remote-controlled pram!" He shook his finger at them. "Babies need looking after all the time. They shouldn't be all on their own, squashed in a pram trying to protect themselves with gamma ray guns and poisonous smoke puffers!"

That was when Miriam came up behind him.

"They wouldn't need to protect themselves," she said, "if you used my idea of having sharp knives sticking out of every wheel."

Everyone stared at her. Except for Tyler, they all looked delighted.

Layla said, "Brilliant idea!"

"You're a genius, Miriam," said Oscar. "I wish you were on our team."

"I can be now," Miriam said. "I wasn't getting on too well, over with that lot."

She looked towards our table, and I looked down, pretending that I wasn't listening.

I could tell Kristy was worried. She said, "But that means we'll have a bigger team than the others."

"No, you won't!" Tyler said. "Because I think your pram is horrible. I don't want anything to do with drawing it. I'm leaving you to go and join their team."

"You'll fit in very well with them," Miriam said. "They have lots of softies over there. All talking about things like furry pram sides and tinkly music and swirly stars."

They all watched giggling, as poor Tyler got up in a huff and stormed across to join our team.

Chapter 8

And the Winner Is ...

Then everyone went quiet and we noticed that the rain had stopped. So Mr Oakway helped us carry the straw bales and our wooden table tops outside.

We settled down to work there.

Robbie and Hetty drew our team's pram with its comfy waterbed mattress.

I coloured in the golden whales and silver dolphins on the mobile.

Sarina drew the musical box. It had a ballerina who spun around as tinkly music played.

Harneesh drew fabulous patterns on the hood of the pram.

Tyler drew four great thick wheels with double brakes for extra safety. And then he added on red parking lights.

Hetty drew soft woolly fingers that popped out to stroke the baby to sleep. Then she added the display of tiny swirly stars to keep the baby happy on dark evenings.

It was a pram that any baby would have loved.

When we had finished, we proudly carried our drawing over to Mrs Hope and Mr Oakway.

The other team took over the drawing of their own pram.

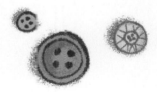

It was so different. It looked more like a missile than a pram. It had guns that stuck out at the front, and a pipe at the back that poured out poisonous smoke. It had a bullet-proof hood and flashing lights all over to warn everyone to keep out of the way. And Miriam had drawn nasty sharp knives sticking out of all the wheels.

"Your pram is so nasty," I heard Tyler mutter.

"So what?" Miriam snapped back. "Your pram is SOPPY and FEEBLE."

We waited while Mr Oakway tried to decide which was best. He hummed and hawed. He kept on saying things like, "I like this!" and "That's very good!" and "Such a clever idea!" and "I would never have thought of that in a million years!"

But we could see that he was getting nowhere. He can never choose. He's just too soft.

We stood there waiting, and we rolled our eyes.

"Hurry up," Mrs Hope told Mr Oakway. She looked at her watch. "The minibus will be here soon to take everyone home."

But still Mr Oakway hummed and hawed. "It's so hard to choose," he complained. "I mean, here is one pram. It's a magnificent machine that goes like the wind and is as tough as a tank. Any baby would feel safe in it, even if they were surrounded by wild animals or crazy drivers or armed bank robbers."

Mr Oakway shook his head in wonder and turned to the other drawing. "But here is the other pram. It's comfy beyond any baby's dreams. It's cosy and warm and chock full of luxury, comfort and pleasure."

We rolled our eyes again.

"No one could choose!" Mr Oakway wailed. "You can't compare two prams as different as these. Each in its own way is a masterpiece of design. They're both quite wonderful. So I'm afraid that they'll both have to win."

I don't think anyone was surprised.
I don't think anyone expected anything
else. As I told you at the start, Mr
Oakway is a total softy and hopeless at
choosing a proper winner.

Hopeless.

So we just made the best of it. After
all, it's not hard to be a winner, even
if everyone else is a winner too. So we
just danced and cheered and clapped
ourselves and said, "Well done!" to our
friends.

That's when Hetty's mum came over the field with Peppo. We fed Peppo fresh grass until the minibus came round the corner. Then we all piled in and waved goodbye to Hetty.

"See you tomorrow!" Mr Oakway called out to us.

"Yes! See you tomorrow!" echoed Mrs Hope. "If I don't pop."

When I got home, my dad asked, "Have you had a good day, Malik?"

"Yes," I said. "Brilliant, thank you."

"Even with all that rain?"

"The rain didn't spoil anything," I told him.

"So what did you do?" Dad asked me.

"We drew a pram," I said.

He gave me a very funny look. "All that time?" he said. "And you just drew a pram?"

"There's a lot more to drawing prams than you might think," I told him proudly. "What we drew would have surprised you! We were the PramBusters!"

I left him staring at me and went off to tell the twins next door about my day at summer camp.

Our books are tested
for children and young people by
children and young people.

Thanks to everyone who consulted on
a manuscript for their time and effort in
helping us to make our books better
for our readers.

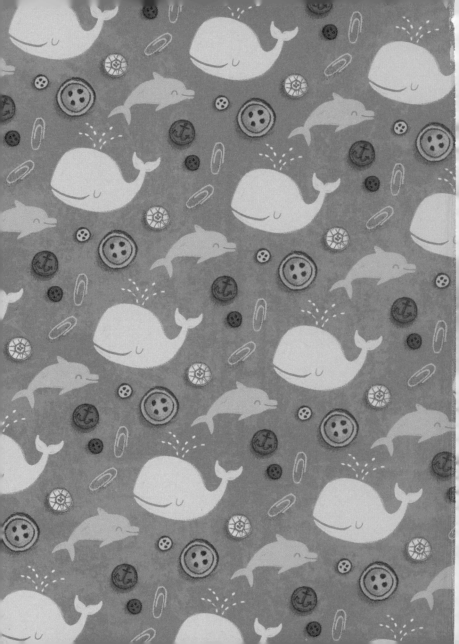